THE OGS LEARN TO FLOAT

Felicity Everett

Designed by Maria Wheatley
and Graham Round

Illustrated by Graham Round

Language and Reading Consultant: David Wray
(Education Department, University of Exeter, England)

Series Editor: Gaby Waters

First published in 1995 by Usborne Publishing Ltd, Usborne House, 83-85 Saffron Hill, London EC1N 8RT, England. Copyright © 1995 Usborne Publishing Ltd.

The Og family lived long ago
in a place called Ogtown.
Their home was a cave.

It was dark and damp, but the Ogs loved it.
Except when it rained.

It had been raining a lot lately.
In fact it hadn't stopped for two weeks.

One night,
the Ogs were gathered
around the old fossil radio
listening to Terry Dactil,
their local DJ.

When suddenly...

THIS IS A FLOOD ALERT!
The River Glug has burst
its banks. Stay in your
caves until you hear
the all clear.

What kind of homework should Zog and Mog have been doing?

But the next day,
Mog and Zog found out
that floods weren't as much
fun as they thought.

They woke up to
find the cave knee-deep
in icy cold water.

One by one,
the Ogs' things were
floating out of the door.

What the...

While the other
Ogs panicked,
Grandma waded in.

*Oh no you
don't, that's my
life's work.*

GRANDMA
OG'S
Recipe Book

MOG
+
STIG

*Grandma,
come back!*

Can you guess which thing
belonged to which Og?

Just as Grandma's recipe
book was about to
float out of sight,
she made a
grab at it.

Only to be swept
into the River Glug.

HELP!

GRANDMA
OG'S
Recipe Book

But Grandma was fast disappearing into the distance.

Mog was afraid that they might never see Grandma again if they didn't act fast.

She rushed off to fetch something useful.

SUPER LONG RANGE TELESCOPE

What was she going to do with it?

Poor Grandma.
She *whooshed*
through the woods...

...and whirled into
Ogtown's high street.

All the town's buildings
were under water,
except one.

Luckily,
Grandma spotted
a bell tower.
It was right in her path.

As the flood swept her past it, she grabbed the clapper and hung on for dear life.

Whew. Saved by the bell.

What building was Grandma clinging to?

Mog thought her bed might be just the thing.

But it sank without a trace.

Zog thought he was on to something...

Bruno's Birthday cake. HANDS OFF! (signed Grandma)

...but it turned out to be a recipe for disaster.

Can you see what Zog was using for a raft?

Then Pa had a bright idea.

He found two sturdy logs from the woodshed and made himself a pair of stilts.

He was just getting into his stride when...

...he lost his balance and crashed into Ma's best china cabinet.

Ma was hopping mad.

Another cave-dweller wasn't too pleased either. Can you spot it?

But Grandpa had a strange smile on his face.

I think I feel an invention coming on.

With that, Grandpa disappeared inside the woodshed.

DINOSAUR DUNG (QUICK DRYING)

Grandpa had never invented
so fast in his life.

But to Grandma
it seemed like a lifetime.

Just as the Ogs were about to give up hope, Grandpa launched his latest invention.

The other Ogs clambered aboard and off they went.

As they neared Ogtown they couldn't see Grandma anywhere.

Perhaps we're too late.

But then Grandma managed to catch Pa's eye. Can you see how?

Just as the Ogs were
heading for home,
the rain clouds started
to blow over
and the

rain

finally

stopped.

Even with Grandma on board,
the Ogs got home in double quick time.
Can you guess what sped them along?

Before long,
the Great Ogtown Flood
was just a bad memory.

And thanks to Grandpa's latest invention,
the Ogs' future had never looked brighter.